Once Upon A Dream

Sweet Dreams

Edited By Sarah Waterhouse

First published in Great Britain in 2024 by:

Young Writers
Remus House
Coltsfoot Drive
Peterborough
PE2 9BF
Telephone: 01733 890066
Website: www.youngwriters.co.uk

All Rights Reserved
Book Design by Ashley Janson
© Copyright Contributors 2024
Softback ISBN 978-1-83685-017-5
Printed and bound in the UK by BookPrintingUK
Website: www.bookprintinguk.com
YB0609E

FOREWORD

Welcome Reader, to a world of dreams.

For Young Writers' latest competition, we asked our writers to dig deep into their imagination and create a poem that paints a picture of what they dream of, whether it's a make-believe world full of wonder or their aspirations for the future.

The result is this collection of fantastic poetic verse that covers a whole host of different topics. Let your mind fly away with the fairies to explore the sweet joy of candy lands, join in with a game of fantasy football, or you may even catch a glimpse of a unicorn or another mythical creature. Beware though, because even dreamland has dark corners, so you may turn a page and walk into a nightmare!

Whereas the majority of our writers chose to stick to a free verse style, others gave themselves the challenge of other techniques such as acrostics and rhyming couplets. We also gave the writers the option to compose their ideas in a story, so watch out for those narrative pieces too!

Each piece in this collection shows the writers' dedication and imagination – we truly believe that seeing their work in print gives them a well-deserved boost of pride, and inspires them to keep writing, so we hope to see more of their work in the future!

CONTENTS

Independent Entrants

Isobel Hedgecock (10)	1
Debbie Wong (9)	2
Keerat Kaur (10)	5
Hafsa Muhammad Nusair (13)	6
Olivia Ellis (10)	9
Isabella Lockwood-Mansfield (11)	10
Robin Ray (8)	12
Shree Patel (10)	14
Victor Umahi Ndiwe (11)	16
Laila Ghannam Begdouri (8)	18
Fatima Khan (12)	20
Nunah Shaw (8)	22
Olivia Quentin-Hicks (12)	24
Daisy Dunning (9)	27
Claire (Jiayi) Liu (8)	28
Bronnie Hyslop (9)	30
Shanvi Rai (12)	32
Shivani Karthikeyan (11)	35
Annika Roy Majumdar (8)	36
Namay Patel (10)	38
Talya Granat (9)	40
Muhammad Qasim (10)	42
Maria Nicolaou (12)	44
Amaya Khan (11)	46
Róża Kalkowska (10)	48
Josee Odaghara (8)	50
Zakiyya Shah (9)	52
Zlata Protsiuk (7)	54
Divishani Iyngaran (10)	56
Rishaan Kumar (8)	58
Zainab Naqvi (10)	60
Milly Kasler (10)	62
Inaaya Umer (10)	64
Melody Nagy (11)	66
Avneet Kaur (8)	68
Joshua Allen (10)	69
Amarachi Obeta (10)	70
Mrigaj Patel (10)	71
Beata Kalthi (11)	72
Armaan Kumar (10)	74
Pone-Pone Htet (11)	75
Sofia Keepa (11)	76
Shilah Wilson Bowden (8)	77
Erine Karenzi (12)	78
Nabiha Khan (11)	79
Eleanor Thomas (10)	80
Vaniya Rai (12)	81
Zaynab Ishola (10)	82
Chiugo Achebe (10)	83
Marion Lim (8)	84
Anouk Shee (10)	85
Eliana Weiden-Laing (9)	86
Priscilla Oke (11)	87
Florence Page-Samuel (7)	88
Abigail Best (10)	89
Amber Clift (7)	90
Maisy Durham (11)	91
Thea Holmes (8)	92
Isabella Roach (11)	93
Merryn Francis (8)	94
Arya Bhatnagar (7)	95
Krishna Pritesh Vadolia (9)	96
Vered Speker (8)	97
Noah Roth (10)	98
Mya Pavey (10)	99
Ivy Emily Mae Mills (11)	100
Olanna Njamma (8)	101
Abigail Yohannes (9)	102
Azima Kanatova (8)	103

Name	Page
Frederick Willow (8)	104
Katrina Tam (9)	105
Danny Gaffori (9)	106
Elizabeth Byford (12)	107
Holly-Grace Sayers (12)	108
Jay Deeljur (9)	109
Mellisa Afram (11)	110
Reuben Worsley (7)	111
Simran Sandhu (9)	112
Arya Lowsley (7)	113
Aesa Springall (8)	114
Sophie Zaraoui	115
Seren Rees (8)	116
Ruby Scudder (10)	117
Keira McKenzie (11)	118
Aycha Ben-Saïd (8)	119
Grace Strain (10)	120
Nancy Rossiter-Pointer (11)	121
Noor Mahmood (9)	122
Theo McGowan	123
Jay Gregory (9)	124
Gracie Gates (9)	125
Lielle Shafran (10)	126
Leila Williams (9)	127
Arisha De Souza (10)	128
Benjamin Corbett (10)	129
Willow May (10)	130
Hope Atkins (10)	131
Oliver Ugurlu (8)	132
Vaani Sodhi (10)	133
Mishika Gupta (8)	134
Emilia Cross (8)	135
Kali Ptolomey (8)	136
Nusayba Ahmed (12)	137
Marilyn Mays	138
Ayaat Khan (10)	139
Lola Clara Stone (7)	140
Bailey Pates (8)	141
Zea Windett (12)	142
Alexander Monk (9)	143
James Edward Young (9)	144
Faith McGowan	145
Hareer Akram (9)	146
Florence Hughes (9)	147
Ashleigh Clayton (11)	148
Alix Chevalier (8)	149
Lennon Morgan (10)	150
Amina Usman (10)	151
Emilia Mahreen (9)	152
Sienna Stanton (10)	153
Yannick Yarro (9)	154
Bea Densley (8)	155
Zoe Chowdhury (8)	156
Tanaya Bharti	157
Primrose Locke (8)	158

THE CREATIVE WRITING

Unicorns

I closed my eyes and felt like I was falling through the air, eventually I landed on a super fluffy cloud. The cloud had pink, blue and yellow colours and almost looked like candyfloss. I slowly picked up a bit and put it in my mouth, it slowly melted, leaving me with a purple stain on my tongue.

Suddenly, there was a huge flash of light, a big creature came down from the sky. It had glittery wings and a pearl-white body with a beautiful rosy pink horn. Slowly, it approached me and flapped its beautiful wings. "Are you a unicorn?" I asked.

The creature nodded and waved her soft, dark pink hair. The unicorn bowed down, letting me sit on her so that we could go for a ride. "Jump onto my back and I shall take you for an adventure to my magical uni land."

We flew past all the other glittering unicorns. We saw all the candyfloss clouds and through the sparkling meadow, I saw a sign saying *Uni Land*.

I met all the other unicorns. I woke up in my comfy bed, thinking, *was this just a dream...?*

Isobel Hedgecock (10)

Save Us!

Save us! Please, save us!
What would you do if your habitat was wrecked?
The crystal-blue sea is glinting in the light
I shook my slippery head, it was polluted
Rubbish was thrown carelessly into the water
Our homes destroyed,
Waste was dumped,
Litter was lumped,
As I stare, helpless at the ruins of our habitat

Save us! Please, save us!
What would you do if you were homeless?
After several long years of misery and imprisonment,
I escape for my freedom
I propel my fins, and travel far and wide,
Finally, I come to a stop
I prop myself up on rocks and stare at a gorgeous, green hilltop
It was a dirty, dark, forgotten junkyard.

Save us! Please, save us!
What would you do if you were in this situation?
I turn around to see a beautiful, bright beach, filled with children's laughter

Playing in the water
Tears swam in my eyes,
I see a clump of children tossing in their picnic waste and running off
I sink into the water,
Unable to defend my habitat

Save us! Please, save us!
What would you do if your habitat was demolished?
I dive into the crystalline ocean,
Now an empty, dark sea filled with garbage
Gilding through the troubled waters
Swimming away from my problems
I swam for days, and days
Save us! Please, save us!
What would you do if you felt trapped?
Eventually, I found a fairly peaceful cluster of shining rocks,
To register my astonishing shock
It was now a filthy mess of muddy rocks.
I rested,
My tail swirling in the water
I feel tired and ravenous
I aqua dive to the now-dirty depths and

Float around, seeking for food
But I found none

Save us! Please, save us!
What would you do if your home was destroyed?
I stare at what was once my home
Reminiscent of the past.
Desperately, I swam back home
I look at the ruins and discovered yet more
Litter scattered across the sea floor
I see bundles of innocent baby whales swimming around helplessly,
Trying desperately to find shelter
I feel powerless, defenceless and alone.
Save us! Please, save us!

Debbie Wong (9)

Fear

When someone mentions their dreams,
Everyone assumes they mean
There are dashing heroes, princesses bold,
Clever animals and tales of old.
But would you like to know what in my mind's eye I see?
Terrible, shocking, as horrible as can be...
I do suppose I don't always see the worst,
But mostly I do, and I might not be the first.

To see familiar faces torn away,
Strong emotions of sorrow and dismay,
People driven mad seeking happiness true,
Turning malicious through and through,

Shattered hopes scattered at my feet,
Witnessing horrors I refuse to repeat,
But there they are, crystal clear,
Haunting me even when loved ones are near.

Always leaving me fearfully quaking,
Whether I be frozen or baking.
A stab at my conscience, an arrow, a knife,
A colossal shadow looming over my life,
Fear.

Keerat Kaur (10)

I Have A Dream

I have a dream that one day, I will soar
Like a bird in the sky, reaching for more
I long to break free from the chains that bind
And leave all my fears and doubts behind

I dream of a world where love conquers hate
Where kindness and compassion dictate
Where we embrace our differences, not shun
And come together, united as one

I dream of a place where children can play
And laughter echoes throughout the day
Where innocence is cherished and preserved
And every child's worth is deserved

I dream of a future filled with hope
Where opportunities abound and we cope
With challenges that come our way
And strive for a better tomorrow, day by day

I dream of a world where justice reigns
Where equality prevails and no one complains
Where the marginalised are uplifted and heard
And everyone is valued, no one ignored

I dream of a life filled with purpose and grace
Where I can make a difference in this place
Where my voice is heard, and my actions inspire
And I have a legacy that will never tire

I dream of a world where peace is the norm
Where conflict and violence are the uniform
Where we lay down our weapons and unite
And build a future that is bright

I have a dream that one day, we will see
The beauty and potential in you and me
And strive to be the best versions of ourselves
And create a world where all dreams can delve.

I have a dream that one day, we will rise
Above the hatred and the lies
And stand together, hand in hand
To build a future that is grand

I believe in this dream with all my heart
And I will never let it depart
For I know that dreams have the power
To change the world, to make it flower

So, let us dream together, you and I
And make this dream a reality, let it fly

For in our dreams lies the key
To a world that is kind, peaceful and free.

Hafsa Muhammad Nusair (13)

Only In My Dreams

When I climb into my bed at night,
And snuggle down under the sheets,
I rest my head on the fluffy pillow,
And I know I am in for a treat!

As I close my eyes and take centre stage,
A mic drops into my hand!
I hear a banging tune and turn around,
And right there is my band!

I roll to the side and take a stretch,
The coloured sprays surround me,
My imagination has gone wild on London's walls,
They've said I'm just like Banksy!

As I wriggle, people start to cheer!
My foot then takes a kick,
They scream my name to spur me on,
Cos I just scored my first hat-trick!

The night starts to fade and the sun starts to rise,
The warm beams through the curtains awaken me,
I'm left with a smile and lots of ambition,
Wondering down which road my next dream will take me.

Olivia Ellis (10)

The Nightmare

I woke with a violent start,
As if after my death someone had shocked paddles into my heart.
Thick layers of sweat coated my face,
I wrapped my blanket around myself, pulling myself into a tight embrace.
I was a wreck who was having a crying fit,
My mind couldn't stop flickering back to it.

'It' being...
My eyes had opened only to find that darkness surrounded me.
Wood boxed up my figure
"Just like she always wanted, buried beneath the oak tree."
Those voices came from above the box,
"Help me..." I croaked, I sounded like a broken record - I needed cough drops.
I banged on the roof of my new home.
Everything came tumbling down: soil, grass, and many fragments of broken stone.
I was underground. Buried alive, you see.
My life was gone, I was never to be free.
I thumped and crashed on the lid,

On deaf ears it fell, those deaf ears couldn't hear the strangled cry of a minor, a young kid!
I kicked and screamed, but still there was nothing I could hear.
Out of my eye came out a large, salty tear.
I kicked the door once more for luck,
Nothing, I was still stuck.
There was nothing I could do.
Stuck and never to get out, that was true.
Free and to go back to school, absolutely 100% untrue.
I drew up all the air in my lungs that I could and I screamed as hard as it would let me.
I woke with a violent start,
As if after my death someone had shocked paddles into my heart.
Thick layers of sweat coated my face,
I wrapped my blanket around myself, pulling myself into a tight embrace.
I was a wreck who was having a crying fit,
My mind couldn't stop flickering back to it.

Isabella Lockwood-Mansfield (11)

Dive Into A Dream!

In this dream, you'll find a fascinating sight that you will fly.
In a dream, there was a beam of light
That struck in front of a team of might,
An exciting creature filled the feature and made this dream madness, with... crazy cream and silver beans even a chocolate delight!
What a unique sight!
But there's more to come as you read on, far away from this amazing land
There was a world of sugar with gingerbread men for a start
And even a biscuit star
And rain, you guessed it, rainbow jelly beans of course!
The clouds are candyfloss
And the gingerbread men have icing sugar frocks.
The trees are lollies and fleas
Well... *anyway*, onto... Celebration Land!
One part is sunny, one part is snowy, one part is, well, cold. In this land
There is Halloween, Christmas, Easter and Valentine's all squished into one island.
In the Christmas part, the snow is fun and all the family have fun opening presents, making gingerbread men and Santa visits every night!

In the Halloween part, all the Halloween spirits come to life, it's such a wondrous sight
You get to see everybody's costumes and get loads of sweets from everybody's house! The Valentine's part has such love, angels fly over the sky
And every day is love at first sight!
The Easter part is probably the yummiest of all! Chocolate every day! Bunnies, chicks and lambs are born every day
As well! *Wow!* A dream full of celebrations, sweets and even magical adventures!

Robin Ray (8)

Once Upon A Time

Once upon a time...

I turned my lights off, yawning
Thinking, *can't wait for next morning!*
Pulled the covers over me
And fell right into a dream

My eyes flitted from side to side
My jaw dropped down, opened wide
As I looked around this wonderland
A cake saying 'Eat me!' in my hand
A mad hatter sipping tea
A well-dressed bunny at my feet

But when I took a step, I felt a tingle
For I was taken away, as fast as the click of a finger
I reached out, but all I had seen was gone
Instead replaced by a shiny glass slipper

The moon was glistening
The wind was whistling
The clock chimed midnight
And a certain prince's face was pale white
A flourish of colours flashed through my mind
Suddenly lay before me a swarm of vines

A ruby-red rose danced in the breeze
As I watched the beast get down on one knee

Now I'm swirling
My whole body is whirling
I land, planted on the ground
Something catches my gaze, spinning round and round
I yell, but it's no use
The princess's arm goes loose
With a prick on her finger, she dwindles
Maleficent laughs, staring at the spindle

I sit upright
Through my curtains seep light
I've woken up from my fairy tale
Taking time to exhale
My story has ended, so it seems
But will I have another dream?

Shree Patel (10)

Once Upon A Dream

In twilight's hush where shadows blend,
A portal opens, realms transcend.
The Dream Weaver spins threads of light,
Weaving worlds within the night.

A castle floats on silver streams,
Built from whispers, born of dreams.
Stars ignite in endless skies,
Mirrored in the dreamer's eyes.

Mountains dance and rivers sing,
In this world where moonbeams ring.
Colours pulse in liquid hues,
Soft as sighs and morning dews.

A forest dense with trees that talk,
Guides the dreamer on their walk.
Paths unfurl like secret scrolls,
Leading deep into their souls.

Figures drift like autumn leaves,
Mumbling truths the heart believes.
Ancient voices, wisdom's calls,
Echo in the dreamer's halls.

In one realm, they soar and fly,
Above the clouds, beyond the sky.
Weightless, free, they twist and turn,
As constellations blaze and burn.

In another, shadows loom,
Whispers of a distant doom.
Yet even in the darkest night,
A spark of hope ignites the light.

The Dream Weaver's touch is mild,
As gentle as a sleeping child.
With each breath, the dreamer sways,
In the dance of night and day.

As dawn's first light begins to creep,
The dreamer stirs from slumber deep.
Threads unwind, the visions fade,
Back to where all dreams are made.

Yet in the heart, a glow remains,
A touch of magic in the veins.
For though the dream may end at dawn,
Its echo lingers, never gone.

Victor Umahi Ndiwe (11)

Once Upon A Dream

Mandy opened her eyes widely, surprised. Her room changed. Mandy jumped out of bed, ran to the bookshelf, the books lying in straight lines, so many colours.

Mandy took one, opened it, started reading. The story was about a little boy, Tony. One morning, Tony went to the forest. Tony met many different animals showing him around, telling how amazing it is to live there and enjoy every day. Mandy stopped reading, placed in the book a coloured feather as a bookmark.

Mandy looked around the room: many different toys. She liked her paper butterflies hanging from the ceiling; they looked alive. Mandy opened one drawer, took a big sheet of coloured paper. She started making a poster of her family. Mandy painted a beautiful rainbow above.

Then, Mandy ran to the doors, opened them, ran across the garden, down to the river. Mandy always liked to come down to the river. Today it was special, so blue. Mandy looked in, saw her shadow. Amazing. After, Mandy heard Mum telling her to wake for breakfast. Mandy opened her eyes, everything dark. Mandy's blind. Very excited, she said, "Mummy, I saw a beautiful dream. I was reading a book, making a poster of our family, going down to the river. Everything was so beautiful! I wish it was real, but it was only a dream." Mandy got a bit sad.

Mum took Mandy on her lap, hugged her tight, whispering in her ear, "I wish your dream one day comes true."

Laila Ghannam Begdouri (8)

When I Close My Eyes

When I close my eyes at night,
I can't help but think and dream,

I am as strong as a tiger,
I ignite like a lighter,
I come powerful and strong,
In my dreams I belong,

When I close my eyes at night,
I am happy,
In my world, there are no fights,
Or time to be grumpy,

When I close my eyes at night,
I would be soaring high in the sky,
Everything in the world would be mine,
Everything would be how it was meant to be, perfectly fine,

When I close my eyes at night,
I know this is my safe space,
A place where I can stay,
And sing all the bottled-up things choked in my heart,

When I close my eyes at night,
I don't have any worries,

And in my world, there are no hurries,
Hurries of the chase of life,
No such thing as only the best shall survive,

I wish my reality was the real way,
Everything was my way,
Everything that I achieved came the easy way,
But I know that's just not the way,

If only I could,
Make the things I see when I close my eyes,
Something I can call my reality,
But deep down I know,
I can't,
No matter how hard I try,

Sometimes there is a spark of hope,
That's what helps me cope,
Don't let anyone take out your fire,
That burns deep inside your soul.

Fatima Khan (12)

Once Upon A Dream, I Dreamt

Once upon a dream,
I dreamt of a world free of harm
I dreamt of a world full of love
I dreamt of a world free of poverty
I dreamt of a world full of hope
I dreamt of a world free of hunger
I dreamt of a world full of smiles
I dreamt of a world free of oppression
I dreamt of a world full of bravery
I dreamt of a world free of injustice
I dreamt of a world full of equality
I dreamt of a world free of diseases
I dreamt of a world full of health
I dreamt of a world free of illiteracy
I dreamt of a world full of knowledge
I dreamt of a world free of pollution
I dreamt of a world full of environmental consciousness
I dreamt of a world free of crime
I dreamt of a world full of justice
I dreamt of a world free of terror
I dreamt of a world full of safety

I dreamt of a world free of chaos
I dreamt of a world full of calmness
I dreamt of a world free of selfishness
I dreamt of a world full of kindness
I dreamt of a world free of war
I dreamt of a world full of peace
I dreamt of a world free of bloodshed
I dreamt of a world full of helping hands
Alas, I dreamt of a child healthy and free, happily paving his way towards an aspiring future.
Once upon a dream, I dreamt of me and of you.
Once upon a dream, I dreamt for us.
Once upon a dream, I dreamt.

Nunah Shaw (8)

My Dream To Be A Writer

If you visit my mind
You can see
All of my thoughts about
Honey and bees

There is a girl named Lola
And a boy named Bob
Who live in a stocking
Down near the bog

You could go see the penguins
Over in Spain
They really love the sun
But don't love the rain

Their kids and siblings
Are living there too
Whereas their parents
Live in the zoo

Say hi to Ruth
Who hates her own name
But I think it's beautiful
All the same

Just don't go to Doubtville
They only speak insult
They live with the bullies
They've started a cult

Then, there's the gate
Reddish and blue
It's only small, but it takes
A while to filter through

And sometimes, people leave
Different to before
Because they got mixed with
Another thought at the door

But that's okay because
I don't mind
If you ignore the doubts
You'll be fine

And sometimes, when
Some thoughts just pop out
It may make a story
That sounds like a shout

But once it is sorted
Into an order

It makes a great tale
To tell your daughter.

Olivia Quentin-Hicks (12)

Dreamland Awaits!

I walk up the stairs to go to bed.
Mummy reads me a story, gives me a kiss on my head.
Snuggling my teddy, I close my eyes.
I'm excited to go to Dreamland up in the skies!

In Dreamland, I dance on clouds with unicorns all around.
I slide down rainbows from the sky to the ground.
With a plop, I land in a big pot of gold!
I wonder if I will be rich when I am grey and old.

Dreamland is such fun because everywhere I go,
There is happiness and laughter and new friends to get to know.
We play tag and we play chess and I win every game!
So, I get to hold up the trophy that says my name.

In Dreamland, I can have afters before main.
With ice cream sundaes and pizza - hooray!
I love going to Dreamland, but now I have to go,
Because I can hear Mummy whispering, "Good morning, hello!"

Daisy Dunning (9)

The Night Sky

Every night, I stare up at the sky,
So many wonderful sights up high.
The first I always see,
Are the stars shining brightly at me.

They sparkle and shimmer like tiny lights,
It feels like they wink at me in the night
And sometimes I see them great,
The beautiful Milky Way like a gigantic state!

It's made up of at least a billion stars,
It really is an amazing sight from afar
And there's the big moon sitting with the stars,
It's so big and bright, you can see it from Mars!

Every night, the moon shines so bright,
It lights up everything in my sight
But sometimes, clouds cover up the moon,
Making everything misty like Neptune.

When the moon covers up the sun, it's cool,
It's called a solar eclipse, and it rules!
The last thing that's rare and so fine,
Are the Northern Lights, they're like a magic sign.

They're exciting and amazing to see,
Mysterious and so pretty to me.

So, every night, when I look out of my window at the sky,
Where these mystical and magical things take place up in the high,
After a while, it soothes me to bed with lovely and wonderful dreams about the night sky.

Claire (Jiayi) Liu (8)

I Had A Dream

I once had a dream, it was crazy as you'll see.
In it was sadness, madness, maybe even gladness.
There were unicorns, pirates, maybe even sirens.
A doctor, a chemist, and a little menace.
Achievement, believement, definitely some grievement.
A friend, a foe, stop whacking lil bro!
A queen, a prince, trying to convince
Me to wake up before the bad dream started.
Finally, my great dream departed, and in it came.
The bad dream had started.
I felt dead.
Like I lost my head.
Suddenly, it changed.
I was squeezed out of my brain.
There I was, in a rusty old chain.
A *prison*, I thought. Had I been caught?
Then, they played a hated song.
Too soon, I got squeezed out again.
No, I was not near any men.
I was... in Big Ben?
The bell chimed and shook me,
I reached for something, and it hit me.
I could wake up! Quickly, I tuned out of the dream, I'd realised I was supreme.

I could escape from this dream-stream.
And out I fell, down on the rug,
Almost knocking over my favourite mug.
I had escaped.
I was great.
I hoped to have that dream again,
So, I picked up my best pen.
I wrote this story, as you will see
For I had a dream...

Bronnie Hyslop (9)

Relief Of An Actor

I drifted off to sleep
And had a dream
In my imagination

Auditions in five
I was in a big situation
The characters assign
Everyone's learning lines
My acting is amateur
Step out of character
There's no going back
You've got to make an impact

It's show day, everyone's preparing
Practising
Running
Rehearsing
Singing
Dancing
Acting
Here comes a lion,
The one everyone loves
The army yells down
An act of defiance

Striking battle drums
The lion frowns

We all retreat
The battle leaves him incomplete

But then, I wake up
This is no dream!
Fox-like make-up
In stage lights gleams
My heart booming
I speak loud and clear
"He has, he has - he has been here!"
The 'animals' are whooping
The evil time is over and gone
Singing a mighty tune
Mr Tumnus, a faun
Calms the large platoon

After the show
After the bouquets
After the overflow
Of the vibrant play
Everyone bellows

Like a mad hatter
I guess this goes to show
The relief of an actor.

Shanvi Rai (12)

My Dreams, My World

I'm going to sleep, tucked up tight,
And I roll over in bed and cry, "Goodnight,"
To be led away from all the qualms in the world,
A small, innocent girl.

To fight dragons, radioactive monsters and
Supervillains inflicting a load of blight,
Saving innocent villagers and
Giving them the gift of hope and light.

Or perhaps to be a rogue explorer,
Surviving tigers and lions and the other mighty roarers.
Making friends with chimpanzees and a monkey,
Who make me quite jumpy.

Or maybe to be a pirate,
And make a riot,
Sailing the seven seas,
While drinking a lot of rum and tea.

You see, every small spark inside your head,
Starts with an idea, a dream,
The amount you can achieve with these thoughts,
Is extreme.

Shivani Karthikeyan (11)

The Magic Box

Based on 'The Magic Box' by Kit Wright

I will put in the box,
A lightning-fast unicorn galloping in fields of gold,
A meandering pathway decorated with wisps of candyfloss,
A rainbow shooting star dashing past me

I will put in the box,
A handful of water from Lake Luna,
A tree alive with rejoicing music from birds,
A house filled with flowers around it

I will put in the box,
The new newsletter for next week, ready to be read,
A shimmer from a slithering snake,
The last joke of a clown

I will put in the box,
A whirlpool of wonder winding me up in wind,
A pinch of lavender, the smell of it so beautiful, so sweet,
The comfort of a cosy duvet warming me up hot

I will put in the box,
Three bleating lambs bleating so loudly I can't hear myself,

The coldness of the Arctic freezing me to death,
The warmth of Africa heating me up warm

My box is fashioned from moonstar-hued ice,
With crystal glittering like sun-lit grains of sand,
On the jewel-encrusted lid and whispers of hope in the corner,
Its hinges are the twisted horn of a unicorn

I shall go riding on a unicorn in my box,
Into the lovely, majestic blue sky,
Then lie on the candyfloss clouds,
And drift into a unicorn world.

Annika Roy Majumdar (8)

Namay's Nightmare

As I drifted off to sleep,
I heard gun noises.
That gave me a shiver down my spine.
I quickly hid under my bed so they couldn't see me.
Then I heard a familiar voice saying, "Namay! Namay!"
Breathing a sigh of relief, I knew my mum wasn't one of the victims of the enemies.
As my mum found me under the bed, she said,
"Pack your bags, we need to get out of here immediately."
"Where is Dad?" I asked, trying not to cry.
She took a deep breath and said, "He's gone out to fight."
My heart sank.
I screamed, "How could you let him fight?"
Courageously, I got out of under my bed.
With a lionheart, I spoke, "I am going to find him."
My mum firmly said, "No.
Thousands of people die in the most gruesome, horrible, and terrifying ways.
I may have lost your dad, but I can't lose you."
Tears rolled down my face.
My eyes blurry.

I wanted to go out there, but I couldn't.
Suddenly, I woke up, I had a petrifying feeling.
I swiftly went to my parents' room.
Dad wasn't there, was this a nightmare or was this real...?

Namay Patel (10)

The Place I Want To Be

When I dream
I dream about a place so high
Dancing in the sky oh so very high
I don't know why
But I am still dancing in the sky
I do ballet, hip-hop and tap too
I don't know about you
But I am dancing in the sky up so high
Dancing, dancing, dancing
The birds chirp, the wind roars
The raven's claws as sharp as a blade
Lightning strikes and thunder awakes
The sun goes away
I am dancing in the sky
But I still don't know why
Ballet, hip-hop and tap too
The sky turns grey instead of blue
The wind starts to scream again
A high-pitched scream
A loud scream
A horrible scream
And down, down, down, down I fell
Out of the sky

Onto the floor
But I am still dancing
Ballet, hip-hop and tap too
Who am I? I'll give you a clue
In fact, I live in the zoo
I have claws too
Squawking and chirping all around the zoo
I don't know about you
But my home is in the zoo
Where I swoop and soar in the sky
Which now turned blue
Remember my clue, I live in the zoo
Who am I? I'll leave it with you.

Talya Granat (9)

Haunted Laughter

In a hotel old and grand,
Ghosts roam its halls so bland.
Friends arrived with laughter near,
Unafraid, they felt no fear.
Creaking floors and shadows deep,
Echoes of their laughter sweep.
Giggling at each spooky sight,
They turned darkness into light.
Midnight snacks and ghostly tricks,
Funny scares and playful flicks.
Ghosts with jokes, oh what a sight,
Haunted delight through the night.
Doors that slam and whispers low,
Objects move, a ghostly show.
Yet their laughter fills the air,
No room for fright, no room for scare.
Master ghost with puns so sly,
Made them laugh until they cried.
In the dawn, they bid adieu,
With hears anew, their memories grew.
From the haunted hotel's embrace,
They left with smiles on their face.
For in the end, they came to see,

Laughter reigns in mystery.
Haunted laughter, echoes clear,
In that hotel they hold dear.
A tale of fun, a tale of fright,
In the haunted hotel of laughter's light.
And there they found their spirits bright,
In the haunted hotel, haunted delight.

Muhammad Qasim (10)

My New World

Drifting off into my imaginary world,
My head on the desk, my thoughts becoming swirled.
Zoning out as the teacher waffles on,
My patience has already gone.

I'm teleported to a wonderful place,
It is far away in outer space,
Vibrant colours of yellow and blue,
This place is too good to be true.

Mythical creatures fly high in the sky,
The glowing plants wave at them as they pass by.
Flowers shimmer and shine in rays of light.
This planet really is a beautiful sight.

Some of the creatures I see have wings,
And others wear crowns, like kings,
Levitating mountains float with ease
Entwined vines swaying in the breeze.

Double rainbows and seven moons,
All the different colours like a peacock's plumes.
Newly discovered animals, from trees they hang
But then, it's back to the classroom with a bang.

The teacher is shouting at me like crazy,
He says, "Will you stop being so lazy?!"
I just want to return to my lovely dream
Where the teacher doesn't lower my self-esteem.

Maria Nicolaou (12)

My Dinosaur

My dinosaur, Fred, although he's cute, is really rather cheeky.
He sleeps on my bed,
He eats all my bread,
He hangs my cat on the pegs,
He tugs at my legs,
He can be very, very sneaky!

One day, he decided to go play with Ned
(Fred's dinosaur friend
Who he liked to offend).
So, he went to the woods
To get some goods -
Eggs to throw at Ned.

Fred slingshotted the egg
Ned's face dripped with yolk,
What a terrible joke!
Ned said, "Fine,"
And climbed up a vine
Fred didn't want to lose his friend, but before he could say anything, along came Greg.

Greg was a diplodocus that loved pasties
He was very cross at Fred

For throwing lots of eggs at Ned,
Greg said, "Apologise! That wasn't very nice.
Let's all become friends again - let's not pay the price,"
And to celebrate, they all ate pasties.

Then, I told Fred to come to bed,
But he goes into my bed again!
He brings Ned and Greg into the bed.
Oh, Fred!

Amaya Khan (11)

Dreams

Come, come to the land of dreams,
Drift through golden gates on soft clouds,
To the wonderful land that gleams
Though it is not what it seems.

Will you come to relax,
On llama-wool chairs heated by dragons?
Or take on the fearsome attacks
Of harpies, or dragons, dinosaurs perhaps?

Should you take on a teacher shift
And teach nymphs and a dancing monkey?
Great elephants will you lift,
Or maybe skyscrapers you'll shift?

Why, the land of dreams is perfect,
Sleeping while having such fun!
You wouldn't imagine how you've just slept
Through such great things that you can't recollect.

Actually, take back the words I said,
I forgot the nightmares, the horrors of sleep,
You'll wake up screaming and shivering in bed.
Forget the nymphs and elephants; you'll have terrible monsters instead!

Although, I think you'll find,
That if you are careful,
Then your dreams will be kind,
And through the golden gates you'll go with ease.

Róża Kalkowska (10)

Magical World

Magical world, glorious it is
Pretty birds
Flying high in the sky
Watching me from the sky

Magical world beautiful to see
Early morning, you come out
Humming words of praise
Across cliffs and rainbow

Magical world filled with
Happiness, kindness, joy
Generosity, peace
This is what makes it a world of magic

Magical world, a place of kindness
Animals and humans help each other
Not eat each other
That makes it a place to stay

Magical world, stay and conquer your fears
Everyone is joyful
Majestic in love and gladness
Make everyone happy

Magical world, silver swans, golden geese

Fluffy rabbits, diamond deers
Iron chickens, bronze rabbits
Place of cute animals

Magical world, place of chocolate
Candy bars and chewy sweets
Snacks so delicious you want more
Make me a place to stay

Magical world, I like you
I am sorry I can't come
Cause you're in my dreams
I pray a portal takes me there.

Josee Odaghara (8)

Once Upon A Dream... Or A Nightmare?

Once upon a dream... or a *nightmare*,
I received a really big *scare*.
It all started with a day at the *fair*,
And I went on a ride, without a *care*.

It turned out to be a terrifying *ride*,
I thought that it would be a *joyride*.
The operator had *lied!*
And I was very *surprised*.

Wild loops and a fire *lit*.
I was scared out of my *wits!*
Monsters snapped and *bit!*
Finally, that was the end of *it*.

I wobbled *away*,
But suddenly, I couldn't see the light of *day!*
The world looked grey, grey, *grey!*
My body transforming into a lump of *clay*.

Abruptly, I woke *up*,
Mother sat on my bed, holding a *cup*,
As well as some *grub*.

As she whispered in my ear, "Don't worry, my little *pup*."

Now I knew that it was all a *dream*,
My smile bright like a big *beam!*

Zakiyya Shah (9)

Kindness Angel's Magic Life

She flies in the air like a pure white dove,
Spreading peace and happiness and all kinds of love.
She wears a frosted white dress with crisp white frills,
And marvellous multicoloured Mukluk boots to keep her tiny toes from chills.
Raindrops and pearls shine like diamonds round her neck,
Her almond-shaped rainbow eyes shower affection and respect.
She's a bright white shining angel with silver wings and snow-white fluff,
With her sunflower-laden basket, she heals the wide world of all bad or evil stuff.
She glows with calm tranquillity and halts all kinds of wrongful things,
Harp music and birdsong sounds can soothe the hearts of kids and kings.
She speaks in every language, but her kindness is her life,
She is tender, sweet and graceful, but above all else, she's nice.
My angel stops all wars and crime and makes the planet safe and joyful,

She heals the world and feeds the world,
I love my angel so much!
She is magical.

Zlata Protsiuk (7)

I Hope Someday...

I hope someday I'll be a shark,
Swimming through the sapphire sea.
But no, sharks eat the live, right?
So sharks are not for me.

I hope someday I'll be an owl,
Fluttering through the beguiling breeze,
And they might take me to their den,
It may be a tight squeeze.

I hope somebody I'll be a deer,
Prancing through the wondrous woods.
But if she had another stag beside her,
He would defeat me if he could.

I hope someday I'll be a meerkat,
Leaping around in the stunning savannah.
But what will I eat there: pizza or fries?
No! I'll be stuck with bananas!

I'll never find the perfect thing,
All my hopes are lost.
Not a shark, owl, deer or meerkat suit me,
I'll go back to being bossed.

But I am a person,
Like everyone here.
I'll have to believe in myself,
Even when fear steps near.

Be a dreamer,
Be a believer.

Divishani Iyngaran (10)

The Fork's Revenge

I hit the fork and the fork fell.
"I won't spare you!" I heard it yell.

"Someone help me!" I felt the pinch.
I sounded like the Grinch.

The poke by his prongs made me cry out a song.
Louder than a roar from King Kong.

I managed to get out of its grip and make a trip.
It followed me to the south; it followed me to the north.

We went round in circles until I became purple.
Seemed like I was running at the speed of a turtle.

It got hold of me and spanked me to the ground
Striking at me as it frowned.

It made me scream
Until I woke from my dream!

I had to check every drawer, every nook.
But there was no sign of the fork with that look.

On the breakfast table, I was having my toast.
The fork's shadow appeared as a ghost.

Taking a deep breath, I grabbed the fork with my might
Locking it far away, out of sight!

Rishaan Kumar (8)

My Dream Of A Special Sight

Once upon a dream, a special sight
A unicorn appeared, shining bright.

It was colourful like a rainbow too
Its mane was soft like a fluffy shoe.

Its horn was sparkly like a shiny light
And its eyes twinkled like the morning sunlight.

With a sparkle and shine, it flew so high
And left a trail of magic in the bright blue sky.

It walked with a smile and a happy face
It brought sweet dreams to a cosy place.

The unicorn was magic, pure and true
And it brought joy to me and you.

It reminded us to dream and never give up the quest
And always believe in the magic of the best.

So, let's dream big and imagine with fun
A unicorn friend for everyone.

If you ever dream of a unicorn so bright
Just remember it's magic and hold on tight.

For in the world of dreams, anything can be true
And a unicorn friend is waiting there for you.

Zainab Naqvi (10)

They Are Coming

They are coming...
Night crawlers
Death bearers
Sleep terrorisers
Mind invaders
Darkness lovers.

They are coming...
Born out of your imagination
Yet uninvited
Hands black as coal
Bound by unforgiving chains
They will never be happy.

They are coming...
Lurking in the darkness of your subconscious
Flanked by a cloak of mist dark as night
Shamed and disowned
Banished to an eternity of despair
Wake is the only escape.

They are coming...
Forgotten in the daylight
Vivid in the darkness

Every move unpredictable
Unstoppable
A trail of mayhem.

They are coming...
Waiting patiently
Eyelids close
The show can begin
Time is muddled
There is no end in sight.

They are coming...
Night crawlers
Death bearers
Sleep terrorisers
Mind invaders
Darkness lovers

They are here.

Milly Kasler (10)

My Majestic Unicorn And Me!

In my cotton candy land,
What do I see?
A bright, magnificent unicorn,
Ambling up to me.
She would spread out her wings,
Which were made out of rainbow and gold.
We would fly in the sky
While she beautifully sings.
The clouds would spy
Whisper while we enjoy.
They would be so jealous of us
Oh, boy! They will splash their tears

Quickly and majestically
The unicorn will say, "Don't panic!
We will fly all the way back home,
Fast with my magic."
We appeared with a tiny *pop!*
We came near the trees.
The lollipops would gather around
While we enjoyed the breeze.
My unicorn would go back to the cotton candy
Eating her lunch.

She would usually gobble it up quickly
Crunch! Crunch! Crunch!
Then, she would snuggle up,
With me and her unicorn friends.
Even if me and the unicorn argues,
Our friendship never ends!

Inaaya Umer (10)

A WWII Typical Day

As I close my tired eyes
And finally get some rest,
Only one thing pops into mind,
WWII and lots of protests.

A WWII typical day
Is different from yours today,
With fighting and death,
You'll lose your breath.

Bombs are thrown all over the place
And sacrifices are always made,
You will probably understand now
That in WWII you are always afraid.

From The Great Invasion Of Normandy
To being a lonely refugee,
Or facing WWII's biggest killer
Adolf Hitler.

Planes, tanks - they were all there,
Jews were not treated right,
They were killed in the harshest way possible
And couldn't *even* put up a fight.

So, now I open my eyes
As the sun begins to rise,
I forget about the war
And get out of my bed - ready to explore...

Melody Nagy (11)

The Lonely Boy

Once upon a time, there was a boy who was alone in the forest. He was wandering around everywhere because he had forgotten the way out.

One creepy, dark night, the boy passed by a haunted house. He was curious, so he decided he would go inside. He went inside but he left the door open so he could go straight out if anything was wrong. But as soon as he went inside, the floorboard started creaking. The door slammed shut. He ran to the door so he could get out, but the door was locked! He was stuck inside. How could he get out? Nobody knew. There were spiderwebs everywhere, including spiders, and his worst fear: snakes.

All the rooms were locked except one, so he went inside. There was a wicked witch! She looked up at him, she was starving. He got the chills! She dragged him in, but he got out through the back door.

Avneet Kaur (8)

Dream Voyage

As he drifted off into a deep sleep, he felt that same sensation he does every night as a wave of sleepiness washed all over him.
The dark and stormy night surrounding his house seemed to be taunting anyone who was outside at this time, but Alex was tucked up cosy in his bed. In contrast to his dream that he had just arrived in, there were clear blue skies dazzled in the eyes of passers-by, yet no sun could be seen, no matter how far one travelled.
At first, Alex felt excited as he did in most of his dreams as he was in control, but little did he know that this was no ordinary dream. Yes, his imagination could run wild, but his darkest fears also could. Why he wasn't in total control this time he was yet to learn; all he knew was that he would remember this night for the rest of his life.

Joshua Allen (10)

The Old Man

I saw him passing by the street as he hauled his shopping bag.
I saw him walking around the farm as he flung the sack over his back.
It made me wonder who he was. Is he new?
I couldn't sleep that night for I wished I knew.

The next day, when I went to school, I saw him by the bus stop, waiting for the bus as I passed him.
Beside him was a little boy, probably the same age as me. I wondered if he could be his grandpa, if not, what was he doing all alone by himself?
It made me wonder who he was. Is he new?
Again, that night I couldn't sleep that night for I wished I knew.

But I didn't need to know...

The next day, they left in a car and never came back. Although I never solved the mystery, it was still fun as it lasted.

Amarachi Obeta (10)

A World I Dream Of

Do you ever think of the world you live in?
A world full of wonders
A world full of bizarre things that come true
Like a roller coaster of emotions,
A place where your mind takes over
Making things you'd never expect,
Where trains will be the journey of your life
And there will be rainbows
Over rainbows
Over rainbows!
I think of a world where sadness ends
Where everyone is equal, rich or poor,
A world where everything is perfect,
A world where climate change is reversed,
Where the ordinary becomes the extraordinary,
Where money grows from trees,
Where birds chirp happily, making a melody
And you can see the notes dancing in the air
As beautiful as the shimmering sea.

That is a world I dream of.

Mrigaj Patel (10)

My Dreams

Soar into space
And reach for the stars,
Or maybe float around
On the famous planet Mars.

Dive down deep into the ocean
Deeper and deeper down you go,
Watching creatures swim by
Ever so slow.

Leap into your fantasies,
A world of chocolaty treats,
A world of candyfloss clouds,
And a world of ice-cream-covered streets.

Maybe something more realistic,
Maybe you go to watch a game,
And meet a world-known player,
Who asks for your name.

Perhaps you dream the opposite
Maybe you want to fight,
As the monster charges at you,
You throw the kryptonite.

Your world turns over,
You begin to fall,
Suddenly, you awake
And you realise nothing has happened at all.

Beata Kalthi (11)

The Snake And The Ant

I am a snake and I fight for my sake.
Look who challenged the snake: I am an ant, tiny but not whiny.

The snake stood to her towering height, ready to bite.
The ant made sure to stay out of sight.

It's going to be tight day and night.
I can't wait till the end of the fight.

The scales gleamed and the fangs appeared venomous,
The snake coiled up, proving to be dangerous.

The ant marched forward with its pointed pincher.
On high alert, not to lose its venture.

The dust blew all over as the snake glided.
And this caused the ant to be blinded.

I stood there, frightened and numb.
How could I be so dumb?

With the impact of the fang and the pincher,
I got out of my slumber.

Armaan Kumar (10)

Unchangeable Past

I close my eyes,
And I slip into dreams.
I imagine myself as a two-year-old boy again,
Being carried by my father,
And when I look at the road,
I see my mother lying on the ground unconscious.
When Father starts to sob,
My two-year-old self realises that Mother is already dead.
As ambulances arrive on the scene, I start to cry too,
For I have lost the person who gave birth to me.
The dream shifts to when I was five years old.
Father, my siblings and I are looking at a letter,
Regarding my older brother's death when fighting in World War II,
I feel nostalgic as I remember all the good times I had with him.
The dream ends and I wake with a start.
I immediately want to go back in time and start afresh,
But I have to accept the fact:
Nobody can change the unchangeable past.

Pone-Pone Htet (11)

I Dream Of A Place

I dream of a place where birds fly free
I dream of a place where you can be
I dream of a place where the stars shine bright
I dream of a place where fireflies dance in the night
I dream of a place where imperfections are perfect
I dream of a place where nature connects
I dream of a place where fish go *whoosh*
I dream of a place where kindness never goes *poof*
I dream of a place that explores other life
I dream of a place that takes it to a whole new height
I dream of a place far beyond the horizon
I dream of a place that glimmers like a diamond
I dream of a place that shimmers like a shooting star
I dream of a place that you don't have to search very far
I dream of a place called... Earth.

Sofia Keepa (11)

David

The one of them all: Sir David, oh David,
He knows everything about nature humans have discovered.
The human king of international nature forevermore;
He'll never stop,
Learning, protecting, searching and connecting.
This naturalist is the naturalist I have always dreamt to be,
I have always dreamt to be like he.

Whales, sharks, fish, scorpions, snow leopards, elephants, Bengal tigers,
Bee-eater birds, black bears, grizzly bears, polar bears,
Penguins, Arctic foxes, long-beaked gannets, eagles and seahorses,
Ravenous orcas, all of these animals he introduces us to.

He is on the right path; a natural genius at being a naturalist.
After all, he is one...

...David Attenborough.

Shilah Wilson Bowden (8)

Starlight's Interlude

To you who live only in my dreams,

Like a star amidst the many wonders of the galaxy
That night will be the first and last time I see you
I long for your return,
Such comfort you brought me in such a small amount of time,
Healing the wounds of my past,
Slipping right out of my grasp.
You tell me I'm special,
That I'm unique unlike any other,
Am I your lover?
Being held in your arms feels so familiar,
Have I been in this situation before?
I can't help but want more.

Your voice is like an interlude,
A break from the havoc and chaos in my mind.
A soothing and heavenly period of time where my mind is at ease,
All thanks to you, my starlight, 'Estel'.

Erine Karenzi (12)

The Motorcycle Race

A *broom broom* sound makes you alarmed!
It's a talent, it isn't easy, it isn't safe, it's just me and that's the way.
Heavy crowd roaring loud, from a distance the fabric sways,
Wheezing through the wind, I flew away.

Fuelling my enthusiasm, conquering all my fears,
Every time I accelerate, I push myself higher, leaving behind,
Ordinary reaching out for the fire.

The thrill of the chase as I speed down the track,
Leaning into turns, never looking back.
The rhythm of the wheels, a melody of speed,
Every day reminding myself that this isn't just a dream,

This is my passion,
This is my need, this is just me fulfilling my ambitious dream.

Nabiha Khan (11)

When I Close My Eyes

I see a magical world taking shape
Beautiful colours fill the landscape
Fizz! Bang! Fireworks light up the sky
I take a deep breath and *wow!* I can fly

Swooping all around, I see a boat
It's covered in pixie dust and starting to float
Beeps and boops are sounding all around
A colossal spaceship lands on the ground

It starts to quiver, it starts to shake
Green aliens emerge with a bright pink cake
Everyone cheers when they hand out slices
To creatures of all shapes and sizes

Like birds in a choir, the sun brightly sings
Around the corner an ice cream van dings
A unicorn hands me a delicious ice
And then... I open my eyes.

Eleanor Thomas (10)

A Fire Without A Flame

Oh, fire that burns so bright,
Your aurora truly highlights your might.
But that is what you miss, your light.
This fire without its glow is not right.
Is it unusual or unseen? Where is the flame?
"A fire cannot lose its flame!" they proclaim
But is their confusion really to blame?
No, yet their answer remains the same.
"This is not to be considered fire if it has no blaze."
Do their answers circle the same maze?
Whoever claims this must be in daze.
Stereotypes really cause thoughts at haze.
It is true, fire can burn with no flame,
The item charcoal is a real claim. Yet there is a fact to blame
Difference cannot be accepted from numerous to name
Because they cannot process what is not the same.

Vaniya Rai (12)

A Dream Beyond The Sky

As I sleep in my bed,
Thoughts of space fill my head,
In my dreams when it's night,
Once dark drowns out the light,
All the planets tell me hi,
As they wave their hands up high,
When I tell them all goodbye,
I realise that I can fly,
There's no gravity after all,
Which means I won't fall,
As I hover to the side,
I see astronauts gleefully glide,
Discovering everything in our universe,
Exploring things vast and wondrous,
Once I land on the moon's surface,
I realise space is wonderful and endless,
When I awake from my slumber,
I lie down, think and wonder,
Why not reach up high,
And dream beyond the sky?

Zaynab Ishola (10)

Thank You, Whale

That night, the sea looked so sparkling,
Its waves dancing in the moonlight, it was glittering
A cool dip in this beauty, she thought
Well, she was out here for a swim, why not?
Splash! In she jumped!
The sea welcomed her as she thumped
But the waves became wild, she first thought it was fun
Though the risk she shouldn't shun
Just as she began to sink
The wonderful whale sprang out within a blink
She was saved, she was so grateful
The kind whale had made a girl so thankful
She rode on his back safely to shore.
Just then, she heard a knock on the door
Her mum's face glowed like a beam
She realised it was just a dream!

Chiugo Achebe (10)

Dream Worlds

I had the best dream ever...
There was a horse
And then the human appeared
Out of nowhere,
Just like that
In a bolt of lightning like someone threw a basketball from the sky.

They fluttered up the soft, white and graceful clouds
Humming and singing,
Like beautiful toy things
They had supper and ate like kings.
They rested on the clouds
All over the bounds.

They went down and down and down
Like super-speedy jets,
They arrived in a sea of trees
Trying to figure out which way to go,
They followed a path which led to a...
Giant Nutella waterfall,
They made comfy beds
And ran across fields of wheat and barley.

Marion Lim (8)

Once Upon A Dream

In all corners of the world, problems rise,
With issues vast, casting shadows so long,
Yet hope springs forth beneath the darkened skies,
Where hearts unite to right the gruesome wrongs.

Oceans plagued by plastic's choking grip,
Now see the hands of many cleanse their side,
And forests burned by the fire's wicked whip,
Regain their green as people turn the tide.

When hunger gnaws at lives in silent pain,
Communities unite to share their bread,
When diseases once spread their evil reign,
New cures emerge, the sick are gently led.

So, let us dream and our actions could prove,
With every problem met, our care can soothe.

Anouk Shee (10)

Why Do I Dream Of Being Alone?

When I close my eyes
The dream comes back again
Depression in my mind
I miss the love, my happiness,
The happiness that gave me the smile I needed
Life is like a box; it opens to feelings, then closes
People leave and forget about you, and you are left alone, no need, no one
I am shut in
No need, no one
My life has lost its spark
No need, no one...

Until... light... A faint image of a door appears in front of me
Should I open it?
Will I open it?
My hand placed on the door
A silhouette of a human lay in front of me and they waved
When I drew closer, I noticed who I was seeing
My only spark...

Eliana Weiden-Laing (9)

Once Upon A Misty Night

Once upon a misty night,
I had myself a dream,
It was strange, fun, full of whimsy,
With magic, cheer and stars that gleam.

I had two very lovely guides,
Of moon and of sun,
They made sure that my trip,
Was very, very fun!

We danced and we laughed,
Our faces full of glee,
I saw all sorts of wonders
As we danced under the trees.

Soon enough they led me
To a field under the stars,
Suddenly, we jumped up
And we were flying past Mars!

They took me to a gateway
Of clouds and of light,
They said their goodbyes:
"We hope you've had a good night!"

Priscilla Oke (11)

Once Upon In Dream Land

Once upon a dream land
Everything was crazy.
Hats were shoes
And shoes were hats
And no one was ever lazy
And ladies were men, and men were ladies.

The world was upside down a lot
Animals wore clothes, and grown-ups were in a cot.

Hearts grew on trees.
They were delicious.
They were as pink as the pinkest roses
And everybody had elephant noses.

Houses were on their side and looked like giant pots of candy.
Ponies did handstands, and unicorns were real, and beaches were not sandy.

In this land, you can be you.
Thank you for coming to my land, I hope it's something new.

Florence Page-Samuel (7)

The Northern Lights

Spinning and dancing, twirling and prancing
With an audience of stars in the sky,
The moon is the judge, she is all silver and white,
They parade through the night like a rainbow of light.

Purples and blues,
Scarlets and greens,
Over the hills and the
Woods and the streams.

People from all over the world
Come to see this miraculous sight,
'Cause this only happens
On a very rare night.

As they twirl and they swirl,
Through the endless night sky,
"Be bright!" they call. "Be keen!" they say.
"Because you will not find us with the sun and the day!"

Abigail Best (10)

Midnight Dreaming

Every night, when I lie in my bed,
All these colours fill my head.
Then, I'm dreaming,
Of flying.

I look down to see,
What's below me.
I give out a shriek,
Now I feel small and weak.

But then, I see I'm dreaming again,
At a speed that no one can gain.
I'm flying on a dragon over a rippling sea,
With a couple of waves below me.

But then, I'm back in bed,
So, I raise my head.
I try to look at the clock,
Then, I realise it's a sock.

I'm up with a start,
Thinking of art,
"That was quite a dream,"
I say with a beam.

Amber Clift (7)

Think, Don't Speak: Dream

Tweedledum and Tweedledee
It's clear to me, you see!
I shall walk along, across a rainbow,
The sky as clear as it can be!
I shall swim across the sea,
Mary Poppins is joining me
I've had nanny after nanny
One was called Nanny McPhee
And so, you see!
My dreams may become reality
It almost seems like wizardry,
Life's a dream
As it seems!
Princesses take me by the hand,
Then take me to a foreign land
Where that will be,
Shall be found out easily
As I wish upon a star,
My dreams shall come true
That star shall travel far
As I wished it to.

Maisy Durham (11)

Forest Fairies

F orever have I loved forests and fairies
O ak trees are magnificent
R ivers glimmer in the sun
E nergy from the forest animals brings the forest to life
S un shining through the trees, buzzing from the many bees
T rees whisper with the gentle breeze

F airies are wonderful
A ll fairies are beautiful
I n the deep of the forest the fairies flutter and dance
R evelling in the beauty of the forest
I nvisible to the human eye
E very little girl's dream is to meet a fairy
S uch special little creatures.

Thea Holmes (8)

A Blast To The Past

D own a whirling spiral.
R ound the corner and down to the floor.
E nd of the journey but where am I?
A n old-looking cottage sat by an old dusty road, with only horse and cart on it.
"**M** aster," said a little girl, "mind the step," but the little girl looked weird, not like a little girl you'd see normally.

A rrived a lady in a beige dress.
W eirdly, I recognised her voice.
A way I went, back through the whirling spiral.
"**Y** ou need to get up; you've got school," spoke Mum, turns out it was all a dream.

Isabella Roach (11)

Flying Bears

Flying bears are pink, flying bears are blue,
Flying bears are just as sweet as you,
Flying bears are magical, flying over you,
You better not eat a cloudberry or everything will glow blue,

Flying bears are soft like a teddy bear,
You better not touch them or else beware!
Flying bears are delicate, delicate like glass,
If you touch them, *smash!*

So, flying bears are clouds,
Don't have the biggest frown,
A smile can never let you down,

So, that's the story of a blue and pink bear,
You will start to glow,
And let everything go!

Merryn Francis (8)

A Smart Boy

Once upon a time, there was a boy named William. He was the smartest boy in class. William was seven years old.

One day, a new boy came. His name was Dan, and William screamed, "Why?" because he found out that Dan was smarter than him.

Soon, Dan asked William to be friends. William said yes because he wanted Dan to teach him stuff.

A few weeks later, William's dream came true. Dan was finally teaching him stuff. But one day, before Dan could teach William eight times eight, Dan moved school because he had found a better school. William was so happy because he was the smartest boy in class again.

Arya Bhatnagar (7)

Phoenix, The King Of Birds

Soaring in the brilliant blue skies,
A firelike bird gracefully sweeps,
As she extends her wings to fly,
I solemnly wave and say goodbye,
Screeching as loud as church bells,
The bird beams proudly.

Streaks of lightning shall not scare her,
The mightiest, the bravest of all,
Her sharp talons are a knife's blade,
A single scratch will tear your skin,
So, beware.

The cuddles are the best and warmest,
Giving you a goodnight's rest,
All for your very own best,
As you see a phoenix, a broad smile
Shall spread across your face.

Krishna Pritesh Vadolia (9)

Lava Dreamland

It was hot!
Sweat trickled down my forehead,
Entering my mouth, forming a bitter taste.
"Aaah!"
I screamed.
Something dragging me by my arm,
Leading me to a towering castle up ahead.
Scrambling,
I saw a glimpse of a monstrous figure,
With horns as big as boulders,
Teeth as sharp as knives grinding together,
Making a piercing screech
Holding tight to the rocky ground
The monster shrieked,
"*Get uppp!*"
I woke up, sweating,
Trembling with fear,
Opening my eyes
Seeing my mother
Hovering above me.

Vered Speker (8)

Noah's Nightmare

Once upon a dream, in the middle of the woods,
It was a dark and stormy night.
The witch in her cellar was cackling,
The wind was howling.

"It's time for dinner,"
She said with an evil laugh.
Her cauldron bubbling, a head floating,
The witch was proud of her creative concoction.

Damp, dark and dingy,
Spooky skeletons hanging from the ceilings,
Smells of sewage wafting around,
Rats and bats everywhere.

"Come here, little boy!"
An ear-piercing scream,
I was awake.
The nightmare was over.

Noah Roth (10)

Deepest, Darkest Fears

Winding down into my deep, deep sleep,
Wondering what genre will make a peep!
Will it be knives? Will it be hives?
Whatever it is, it will give you a fright!
(Maybe too much, you'll have to sleep with the light)

Bees, trees, windy leaves.
They're so small, you won't realise they're below your knees.
Little, small and scared,
You have to make sure there's nothing under your bed!

Perhaps you will be saved by the morning sun?
You better keep running, run, run, run!
The dark black night draws on and long,
Please let me wake and be free from then on.

Mya Pavey (10)

Bad Dreams

It was just a bad dream
Everything's alright
It was just a bad dream
Although you felt it tonight
It was just a bad dream
Even if you forget it
It was just a bad dream
No matter how you regret it
It was just a bad dream
Nobody can hurt you
It was just a bad dream
He didn't desert you
It was just a bad dream
You just wanted to yell
It was just a bad dream
But still you didn't tell
It was only a bad dream
There was no danger or gun or knife
Until you sat and realised those dreams are your real life.

Ivy Emily Mae Mills (11)

Stars

When I feel alone, I look up at the stars,
Celestial,
Dancing in the shimmering moonlight,
An awe-inspiring sight,
That fills me with delight,
In the darkest of nights.

When darkness overcomes the night,
Like a blanket covering the light,
Then, the stars come out so bright,
Diamonds in the sky.

The galaxy, an endless place of curiosity, excites me,
One day, I might visit space,
See the stars up close,
But the stars are so far away,
So for now, I will watch from a distance,
And smile as I think of their wonder.

Olanna Njamma (8)

The Night Of Horror

I was in this wonderful world.
Far better than the new one.
I smiled like I never smiled before
But that smile didn't last for long.
I bumped my head hard on the
Ground and when I looked up
I was in this devastating world.
I started to look around to see if
I was maybe dreaming in my dream, but this wasn't it.
I got chased, chased to the end of the world, but then I woke up
It was a normal day, I went to school like always
When I came back, I slept again and this time it said

'I *will* hunt you down!'

Abigail Yohannes (9)

A Witch's Unpleasant Life (Dream)

If we go back in time,
To see the witch's irksome life
Maybe you'll learn so much,
That you'll have pity in your heart.

Once upon a time,
There lived a lady, Madeline.
She was kind, generous and beautiful,
But she had an abundance of furies.

Because of lots of furies,
She became a monstrous witch.
Her life will suffer just like this,
If she continues this behaviour.

I woke up in the morning,
Screaming and in pain.
Then, I realised it's a dream,
A silly, fictional dream.

Azima Kanatova (8)

I Had A Dream Of Blu-Tack

My house is made of Blu-Tack,
So I asked my friend for some,
Because my door had stretched
When I pulled it with my thumb.

The Blu-Tack stretched so tight
When I let it go, it went *zwing!*
It was floppy enough to collapse
As it plopped on everything.

When I asked for some,
My friend said, "Why?"
"I need it for my house!" I said
And I felt really shy!

She gave me a blob of Blu-Tack,
I went home to fix my door,
I was so disappointed
My house was a dinosaur!

Frederick Willow (8)

My Dream Of A Home Dome

In my dream, there is a house,
That is shaped like a dome,
I call it a home dome.
It is big,
Like a giant pig,
With a shower that smells like Jasmine powder.
Full of calmness and happiness,
Everyone will enjoy it with grace,
It stays still,
Like a huge well,
But how loud it is when the winds rustle,
If you enter the inside of it,
I wonder if I were the dome,
What would I do?
I decide I will sleep in a deep dream.
In my dream, there is a house,
That is shaped like a dome.
I call it a home dome.

Katrina Tam (9)

One Boy's Dream

Once upon a starry night,
There stood a boy flying his kite,
He sighed as he played in the cold winter air,
"If only I could fly like my kite up there."
He soon went to bed and read a book
And so, it came to him like reeling a hook,
"I shall be an astronaut and fly in a rocket!"
Then, he reached into his pocket,
And brought out a toy,
"I know I am a boy
But when I'm a man
I will step foot on the moon land."
Although this is only a boy's dream,
He shall always be keen.

Danny Gaffori (9)

I Closed My Eyes

I closed my eyes and:

D arkness became light,
R ejection became acceptance,
E nemies became friends,
A nxiety became hope,
M eanness became kindness,
T he impossible became possible.

I opened my eyes and:

A sked to volunteer at a charity bake sale,
C arried my cousin on the mountain trail.
T ried hard to be kind, not to be cool,
E mptied the rubbish bins at my school,
D id a charity swim at my local pool.

Elizabeth Byford (12)

Wishes For My Sister Mary

Dream big, little star.
I hope you'll drive a red car.

Dream awesome, smiley star.
Together, we'll go far

Dream like me, little Mary
You definitely could be the kindest fairy.

Dream like Toby, Miss Mary
Gaming, maybe sharing and caring.

Without the long moustache!

Mary, you're very cheeky, very cute
I love you.

I am of course amazing, pretty, intelligent and wonderful.
I hope you are too

Let's go on our dream
Adventures together!

Holly-Grace Sayers (12)

Your Greatest Fear

What's your greatest fear?
Is it sharks and snakes
Or orcas and octopuses,

Scaring and screeching and
Scratching and scampering?

They'll haunt you and frighten you
Until you scream and yelp for help.

You'll turn off the light and say goodnight
But you find that it's no use at all,

The next night, they'll come back again,
Creepy and crawly, stealthy and surely,

So, just slap yourself, you silly old child
You'll be awake in a little while...

Jay Deeljur (9)

Haunted House

I think there's something moving
Over by that chair
But when I take a closer look
There's really nothing there
Oh, look! What shot across the room?
That gave me such a fright
I hate being alone
Especially at night
Now there's something creaking
It's the bedroom door
Oh, I really hate this house
I'm not staying anymore
I know I'm really nervous
But the thing I hate the most
I shouldn't be so frightened
'Cause I'm the *ghost!*

Mellisa Afram (11)

I Dreamed Of Solving A Rubik's Cube

When I learnt how to solve a Rubik's cube
I found it very hard
I kept turning the whole cube
Instead of turning half

It didn't take long to learn
It took about a week
I kept getting frustrated
And got quite annoyed

But then, one day, at seven
I did this very thing:
I solved the Rubik's cube
And did it all in bed

Now I can solve the Rubik's cube
I can do it really easily
I can also do it really fast
My record's twenty seconds.

Reuben Worsley (7)

A Dreamy Melody

My leaf looks like an eagle's wing,
My leaf smells like a chocolate string,
My leaf feels like a diamond ring,
My leaf reminds me of a time in spring.

My feather looks like a steaming kettle,
My feather smells like a rose petal,
My feather feels like a frozen metal,
My feather reminds me of the day I'd settle.

My dream looks like an envelope seal,
My dream smells like an orange peel,
My dream feels like it is real,
My dream reminds me of my adventurous deal.

Simran Sandhu (9)

The Unicorn

U nder the stars, a unicorn smiled as she saw a shooting star,
N ight-time is when the unicorn's magic increases,
I ts glistening mane shimmers like a silver waterfall,
C aught in the shine of moonlight, the unicorn's enchanting bright eyes are wide open,
O n the lush green meadow, the unicorn searches for new unicorn friends,
R eflected in a puddle, the unicorn saw another unicorn grazing,
N ow the unicorn had a buddy and they were together forevermore.

Arya Lowsley (7)

Dragon Dreaming

Dragons soaring through the sky,
Only when I close my eyes.

Mythical creatures float through the clouds
Mighty, immortal, fang and claw.
Peaceful moonlight glows, soft, ethereal
Dragon shadows glide, quiet, calm.

Spirits of the wise whisper their secret songs
Calling to the dragons of hope and joy.
Bright starlit night, still, luminous
Ancient lullabies soothe, gentle, tranquil.

Dragons soaring through the sky
Only when I close my eyes.

Aesa Springall (8)

Last Night I Thought I Was Dreaming

Last night I thought I was dreaming,
Computers played gaming games and completely had fun dancing in duets like dancers.

Last night I thought I was dreaming,
Messy whiteboard all over it waiting, waiting, waiting to get scrubbed off.

Last night I thought I was dreaming,
Angry vacuum hummed like a monstrous king bee, sucked up all the litter.

Last night I thought I was dreaming,
Trays raced with magic pens then had a sleepover and had a pillow fight.

Sophie Zaraoui

Candyfloss Miracle

Alice takes some baths,
I do some boring maths,
We go across some paths,

We get all the way across,
There's a house made of candyfloss,
There are some walls full of moss,

The lady is very kind,
She never ever minds,
Because she is a bit blind,

Then, she did a spell with a wink,
And got out some pink ink,
Then, Alice's hair turned pink,

On the way back,
Alice did a whack,
There were lots of cracks.

Seren Rees (8)

A Ballet Dream

Once upon a ballet dream,
There was a girl who found her theme,
She danced all day, she danced all night,
But then she got a little fright,
She tried her best, she tried all day,
But little Charlotte had nothing to say,
She had a competition coming up,
But she knew she couldn't give up,
When the competition came,
She knew it was her chance for fame,
She made it her best,
She opened her chest,
Then she danced, she danced, she danced.

Ruby Scudder (10)

Monsters In My Head

Creeping, crawling in my head,
The darkness overwhelms.
Grabbing, yanking, pulling me into the depths of despair,
Chained to a wall that is somewhere far from help.
The ludicrousness of it all makes me start to laugh,
Until I see them coming.
Now I know why I am here,
What I am doing.
Kidnapped from the tales of princesses and happy endings in my sleep;
Dragged to the abysmal dungeons instead.
They are here.
And there is no escape.

Keira McKenzie (11)

Dream Town

Don't like school?
Then you don't have to go, it's really up to you.

We have holidays for everyone,
Gamers, explorers, sleepers, foodies and footballers.
The list goes on.
If you're bored of the same old holidays, come join the fun.

Infinite burgers. They fall from the sky.
We have all the food you can imagine, come give it a try.
Pizza, ice cream, crisps, *oh my!*

Come and join the fun! See you there.

Aycha Ben-Saïd (8)

Horse Rider

My dream is a dream I really want to come true
Although it is harder than it may look
I want to be a horse rider jumping over jumps
But my pony is a little dumb
All I need is a little leg power
To finally be on top of the judge's tower
I am going to try and try until I get there
Everyone says we are a great pair
We both are lazy and very crazy
One day, I hope to reach my dream
And the next time I see him, I hope he is clean.

Grace Strain (10)

Stories

Cups of tea and a bucket full of stories

"It's cosy by the fire."
"Why don't I take you to a land without so many worries?
The Three Little Pigs and the Three Blind Mice all think six is much more nice.
The three musketeers helping George slay the dragon,
Jack and Jill running up the hill, carrying a flagon.
All the princes, Rapunzel in her tower."
"That made it so much cosier by the fire."

Nancy Rossiter-Pointer (11)

Cotton Candy Clouds

Once, I had a dream,
I lived on the clouds,
Cotton candy seems to be all around.
Pink and purple; sometimes blue,
Munching away, *chew, chew, chew.*
On my cloud, country is the perfect view,
There will be cotton candy all around you!
But I wake up to find,
The dream isn't true,
I'm just in my bed, hoping my dream will be new,
But I'm glad to be awake,
And to see my mum smile down at my face.

Noor Mahmood (9)

Mysterious Night

In my spooky dream, there is a mist
That can be seen, but when I get closer
I fall down a stream
But I can't see anything
Then I hear a creak, in the darkness it is freaky.

I travel through the shadow realms as well as tumbling down,
Through the misty night, I see a mysterious fight
But it is no ordinary fight, it is tight and light
The adventurist warrior looks up to the galaxy above
Never to be seen again.

Theo McGowan

Giraffes

I want to be a giraffe
As small as a calf
Walking on the path
Doing some maths,
That would be a laugh.

Spots on my coat,
As small as a goat
With a very long throat
That floats my boat.

I can't touch the trees
Or even other giraffes' knees.
Oh, yes please.

Playing with the chicks
Doing mathematics tricks
While the other giraffes
Are collecting sticks.

Jay Gregory (9)

Dreamland

A mysterious day in Dreamland,
A kaleidoscope of flowers floats through your hair, singing, "La la la."
Dazzling skies as blue as a shimmering sapphire.
Flying, playful pandas tumbling around you say, "How do you do?"
Glimmering grass as green as an emerald,
Soft, pillowy moss like a blanket under your feet.
Delightful candyfloss trees surround you,
But watch out for the cantankerous troll!

Gracie Gates (9)

Memories

Memories going through my head,
While I'm dreaming in my bed.
Some might bring me joy,
Some might just annoy.
Some might just make me sad,
And some might make me mad.
Along the path to memory lane,
Where all the memories are in my brain.
Swishing and swirling around in my head,
It is impossible to get to bed.
All I can hear are people talking,
And now my brain is terribly falling.

Lielle Shafran (10)

Dreams And Wishes

I wish I could transform and become a leopard someday,
For everyone to be friends and wish their troubles away,
I like to play Minecraft and Concrete Genie too,
But my dream is to be an artist. How about you?
Family and friends are very important to me,
I wish we could all live happily for eternity,
All of these things would be like a dream come true,
I hope they will one day, for me and for you!

Leila Williams (9)

Dreaming

D reaming takes you away from reality
R ealms and different worlds beyond your wildest dreams
E verything so real yet so imaginary
A ll things good, all things bad
M aking you quite happy or quite sad
I maginations going wild
N ot remembering anymore if you're adult or child
G et up! Get up! You're late for school! And make sure to be kind!

Arisha De Souza (10)

Dragons And Beyond

In a magic land where dragons soar,
Your sharp eyes meet a tiny door;
Now please do note that you are not Alice -
In fact, you are in a towering palace!

You are in a place that's beyond your dreams,
Beyond your nightmares, beyond your screams.

A dazzling dragon flies towards you roaring,
But just then, you find yourself soaring,
Back into your comfy bed -
You much prefer real life instead!

Benjamin Corbett (10)

Willow

W hispering in the calming midnight breeze,
I n a valley full of different trees,
L ong, bright leaves and branches,
L onely when it dances,
O ne different, isolated shrub,
W illow.

Lost in the whispering darkness,
In among the unknown.
Lingering in its own sharpness,
Following as it was shown,
In the darkness, all alone.

Willow May (10)

Flying Cat

A cat going to space in a rocket ship
Flying in the air above, is it a cat or a dot?
On the moon, eating treats
A grey cat flies in a rocket ship to meet his friend on Earth.
The grey, amber-eyed cat wants to go to space.
His happy place is the moon.
The black cat wants to go to Mars, but people say no.
The black, green-eyed cat goes to space with the grey cat, his best friend.

Hope Atkins (10)

The Poet Tree

P oet trees swish their poems around.
O nomatopoeia is key in the poet tree.
E lephants trump around the poet tree.
T rees are unlike a poet tree.

T antalising words fall off a poet tree.
R oots grow deep beneath the surface.
E vergreens have a new species, the poet tree.
E ternally, words will grow on the poet tree.

Oliver Ugurlu (8)

I Met Her

Once upon a dream, I met her.
She was so sweet and kind.
So funny and brave.
We've been together my entire life.
We went on adventures.
Faced our fears.
And treasured our special things.
We did the same things.
Went to the same places.
And made the right things happen.
Never for an instant had I known,
That that little special girl,
Was me.

Vaani Sodhi (10)

Mental Health

M y (our) voice matters and
E verybody counts
N othing is impossible as
T omorrow is a new day for
A ll of us with
L ove all around

H appiness is the cure and
E verybody's solution
A ll of us together
L iving, loving and laughing
T his year with
H ope in our hearts.

Mishika Gupta (8)

Once Upon A Dream

Deep in a book, adventures will seek,
Beneath your eyes, the darkness will see.
Frightening noise came your way,
Beneath the dark shadows, someone lay.
One by one, someone is out,
You will trip all about into one big shout.
Adventures can see as much as a bee
But what does that mean?
Bees in a dream can make it complete
So, what can you see?

Emilia Cross (8)

Wondrous Dreams

Once upon a dream,
On a cold, dark winter's night,
I was snuggled up in bed,
My mum just turned out the light,

I close my eyes and drift away to far-off distant lands,
So strange and full of lots of stuff I do not understand,

I could be a princess, or a fairy shining bright,
Who knows what adventures wait for me when I sleep tomorrow night?

Kali Ptolomey (8)

Dreams

Residing on your pillow,
When stars twinkle in the sky
Embracing you into a new world
As you close your sleepy eyes
Filled with wonder and excitement,
Sometimes magical, bright like the night moon
Or creeping in your mind like dark shadows,
That send upon you cold shivers
Awaiting you each night,
Adventures unknown,
Where will your dreams take you?

Nusayba Ahmed (12)

The Forest

I like to be in the lush green forest, with beautiful birds singing and rivers murmuring.
Bright green moss under my feet and the sunlight filtering through the trees, making them glow.
Vibrant yellow butterflies with their wings shining.
Green everywhere I look, and a cool breeze drifting through the leaves, making them dance and wave.

Marilyn Mays

Lost In The City

I took a wrong turn
Mum, where are you?
Lost in the crowd, a city so big
Buildings so high, covering the sky
Droplets of rain
So cold and alone
I'm scared
You were just there and now you're not.
Tears falling, standing still
Feeling small
Mum, Mum, where are you?
Mum, I'm scared.

Ayaat Khan (10)

Nightmares

Nightmares, nightmares, get all cosy in my bed
Nightmares, nightmares, cuddle up with my ted
Nightmares, nightmares make me scared and feel so sad
Nightmares, nightmares, my body starts to feel bad
Nightmares, nightmares, I get anxious and want to run away
Nightmares, nightmares, I wake and hope I have a better day.

Lola Clara Stone (7)

The One Roller Bird Poem

There is a bird
On a branch, that says,
"Tweet, tweet."
He mostly likes to
Fly and eat.
Maybe worms or slugs
Or snails? Who knows?
In a tree, on the
Nice branch, he shows
Off his feathers
And does a
Pose.
The bird,
The bird, it's
A colourful bird.

Bailey Pates (8)

A Place Where Life Will Never Live

Just like dreams,
Nightmares can come true,

Turn lives of pain,
Into ones no one wants to live,

Drain good memories,
Highlighting ones of bad,

I was falling,
Falling,
Falling,

Into a deep pit of never-ending darkness,
A place where life will never live.

Zea Windett (12)

The Dream Of Snow

The dream weather, snow,
The white miracle,
The wonder of the sky,
It's like lots of little blankets,
But just too fragile,
Many countries don't have it,
Some always have it,
But some sometimes have it,
Some people love it,
Some don't,
Which one are you, sun or snow?

Alexander Monk (9)

Dream

D reams are amazing, go to sleep then you'll agree!
R eally, the only limit is your imagination!
E xamples might be what you need?
A dream wouldn't have them as they're whatever you need them to be!
M ost people love dreams, have one and see why!

James Edward Young (9)

Me And The Snow Leopard

I go to the icy Arctic,
There's a magical snow leopard,
Right in front of me.
She has white fur and sparkles, I can see,
I ask the snow leopard, "Would you like to be my friend?"
She says, "Yes, until the end."
We play in the snow, until I have to go.

Faith McGowan

My Many Dreams!

I dream to be a lawyer
Although I know other jobs are funner
I dream to have an enormous house
Not one as tiny as a mouse,
I dream to use my skills in poetry,
In my opinion, it's like a speciality
I dream to help others
And still care for my sister and brothers.

Hareer Akram (9)

I Love To Dance

There is one thing that is always on my mind
It's to dance in the West End.
The sparkly, bright, colourful dresses and
Their absolutely outstanding, beautiful wigs.
Dancing their hearts out
Maybe, one day, if I keep working hard
My dream will come true.

Florence Hughes (9)

Fairies Dance!

Fairies dance.
Fairies prance.
Watch them twirl.
Watch them whirl.
See them skip.
They never trip!
See them sway.
Well on their way.
There they go.
Their hair aglow.
Off they dance, into the day.
Maybe I'll come back in May!

Ashleigh Clayton (11)

A Dream

We all have dreams.
Some are big and others small
But you have to choose one
Because you can't have them all.

In a dream, you see colours bright
And in a nightmare, you feel fright.
Which one will you choose?
I hope it is good news.

Alix Chevalier (8)

Money's Not Edible

As the markets expand...
The fires follow suit,
As the people buy...
The creatures die.

As the factories pump...
The planet becomes a dump,
As we run and hide, we regain the memories...
Of all of the human race felonies.

Lennon Morgan (10)

Once, In My Dream

Once, in my dream
I saw a pretty scheme
In there were flowers
And I had superpowers
In there, I was flying
And it was very exciting
I could hear a cat
She purred in a hat
Once, in my dreams
The end of my schemes.

Amina Usman (10)

Dreams

D estinies are planned!
R esilience is required!
E ncouragement helps a lot!
A nxiety is pushed away!
M otivation gets us going!
S mall steps become big steps!

Emilia Mahreen (9)

Grayson!

His name is Grayson
People call him Jason
It makes him purr
When I brush his fur
He's fun to squeeze
Easy to tease
He's proud
He's loud
My lovely Sable Burmese.

Sienna Stanton (10)

Dawning Moon

D awning moon
I ncredible scenes
S un out of sight
T errible darkness
A rmy of stars
N othing but darkness
T ranquillity remains.

Yannick Yarro (9)

Once Upon A Dream

I was flying in the sky
Clouds beyond.
Whirling and twirling
In the air
Glistening stars
Sleeping on fluffy clouds
Wonderful life beyond.
Everyone staring up at me.

Bea Densley (8)

The Daffodils

Yellow, mellow daffodils,
Swaying and shimmering
On the green grass.
Dancing like peacocks,
Standing like soldiers,
As quiet as mice,
Beautiful big daffodils.

Zoe Chowdhury (8)

Myself

M y kind grandma
Y ummy pasta
S wimming is fun
E xcited people at school
L ovely marshmallows
F unny pandas.

Tanaya Bharti

Winters

Winter
Creeps
In
Night-time is here,
Time to dream,
Exciting things inside my head
Real or imagined?
Snow and ice
Ski and slide,
Speeding, sliding.

Primrose Locke (8)

YOUNG WRITERS INFORMATION

We hope you have enjoyed reading this book – and that you will continue to in the coming years.

If you're a young writer who enjoys reading and creative writing, or the parent of an enthusiastic poet or story writer, do visit our website **www.youngwriters.co.uk**. Here you will find free competitions, workshops and games, as well as recommended reads, a poetry glossary and our blog.

If you would like to order further copies of this book, or any of our other titles, then please give us a call or visit **www.youngwriters.co.uk**.

Young Writers
Remus House
Coltsfoot Drive
Peterborough
PE2 9BF
(01733) 890066
info@youngwriters.co.uk

- YoungWritersUK
- YoungWritersCW
- youngwriterscw
- youngwriterscw